The subject ma and
vocabulary hav
with expert assistance, and the
brief and simple text is printed
in large, clear type.

Children's questions are
anticipated and facts presented
in a logical sequence. Where
possible, the books show
what happened in the past
and what is relevant today.

Special artwork has been
commissioned to set a standard
rarely seen in books for this
reading age and at this price.

Full-colour illustrations are on
all 48 pages to give maximum
impact and provide the
extra enrichment that is the
aim of all Ladybird Leaders.

A Ladybird Leader

castles

Written by John West
Illustrated by Frank Humphris

Ladybird Books Loughborough

Before the days of castles

Men have always needed a place
where they could be safe.

A cave on a hillside
could be a safe place.

Cave men were often
attacked by animals.

They defended themselves
with fire, sticks and stones.

An earth fort high on a hill

Later, the attackers were other tribes.
Hill tops were made into forts.
Ditches were dug round them
and wooden fences built.

An Iron Age fort

Maiden Castle, Dorset

The remains of this old fort
can be seen near Dorchester, England.

It is about ½ mile (.805 km) long.

It has deep ditches and earth banks
as high as a house.

A stone city of Ancient Greece

The Acropolis in Athens

This picture shows part
of a very old Greek city.

It is on a rock 500 feet (152.4m) high.
There was only one way in.

A village over water

Some very early villages
were built over water.
An enemy could reach them
only by boat.
Villages like this
can still be seen in Borneo.

A Roman fort

The Romans gave us the word for castle.
They called this fort a 'castrum'.
3,000 soldiers lived here.
A castrum had strong walls
with gates, towers and a ditch.

How places became safer

A deep ditch and bank helped to keep attackers away.

A wooden wall was safer.

To build on a cliff edge by water was safer still.

Best of all was to have water all round.

A village inside a wooden wall

Some people built stone walls.
Others still used wood.
The sharp stakes kept attackers
out of this Saxon village.

Another village
inside a wooden wall

Africans, too, put fences
around their houses and animals.

Like the Saxons, they built houses
with mud, straw and wood.

A Norman castle of wood

Norman knights built the first castles.

These were in France.

They made a little hill of earth
and put a wooden tower on it.

This picture is part of the famous Bayeux tapestry.

A Norman castle of stone

Later, the Normans built some stone
castles in France, England, Scotland,
Wales and Ireland.

A castle built by Crusaders

When the Normans fought in Palestine,
they were called Crusaders.
They built castles there and in Egypt.
The ruins are still there in the sand.

Defending a castle in the Middle Ages

The drawbridge was pulled up.

Then the portcullis gate came down.

The first attackers were trapped.

Hot ashes were poured through holes in the walls.

Inside the walls were more walls.

An archer stood at every slit in the walls.

Capturing a castle

Large, wooden machines were built.

These worked as catapults and threw huge stones.

Heavy tree trunks were used
to break down castle doors.

Wooden towers and ladders were
used to climb over walls.

Holes were dug under walls.

Towers

A square tower
is called a keep.

These are often
called drum towers.

Do you see why?

Church towers were often like castle towers.
Sometimes the church was the safest place in the village.

Ships with 'castles'

In the Middle Ages, ships were built
with wooden 'castles' at each end.

The front part of a ship's deck
is still called the forecastle.

(pronounced fo'c'sle)

A 'fairy-story' castle

This was a real French castle.

It was like a fairy-story castle
for a princess or giant.

The towers were round and had
tall spires.

A fortified farm-house

Some farm-houses needed strong walls
to defend them against raiders.
This one was a small manor house
of the late Middle Ages.

A ruined castle

Many castles today are ruins.
The picture also shows what
this castle once looked like.

Walls around towns

A walled town
in France

Some towns had walls around them.
These can still be seen in Europe.
In Britain you can see them
at York, Chester and Conway.

Walls between countries

Hadrian's wall
(near the Scottish border)

The Romans built this wall
to keep the Picts out of England.
It was 73 miles (117 km) long.
There were small towers and forts
along it.

The oldest wall to guard a country
is the Great Wall of China.

It is 2,000 years old
and 1,500 miles (2 414 km) long.

Cannons that broke down castle walls

15th century

16th century

17th century

The first cannons were used about 600 years ago.

Towers by the sea

Martello towers like this were used
to guard the coast of England.
They were built 200 years ago.

A 19th century fort
in the United States

Forts like this were used
by American soldiers
about 120 years ago.

The Indians had no cannons
to break down the walls.

A Russian fort

This was the fort of Sebastopol
in 1854.
The French and British
could not capture it.

Forts became less important

Forts became less important.
Armies marched round them.
In 1870, the Prussians reached
Paris in this way.

The arrows show how it was done.

A moving fort

A tank is really a moving fort.
This was one of the first tanks.
It was used in 1917,
in the First World War.

The Maginot Line

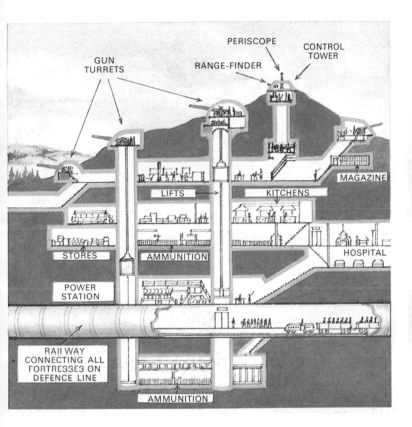

Early in the Second World War,
French soldiers lived in forts like this.

They worked, ate and slept
under the ground.

Defending a modern town

In the Second World War,
bombers attacked towns.

Wires hanging from these balloons
made a kind of wall to stop them.

The aircraft could not get too close.

In olden days, defenders on castle walls watched for attackers.

Today, enemy aircraft and rockets, hundreds of miles away, can be shown on a kind of television screen.

A fort in the desert

Some French soldiers lived in forts
like this in the desert.

They were in North Africa.

How some castles are used today

Many castles are still in use today.
This castle in Cardiff
is used as a college.

In the past, some rich people built mock, ruined castles.

These were called follies.

The people thought that follies made their parks more interesting.

In the days of Queen Victoria,
some houses like these were built.
They were made to look like castles.
The owners felt more important.

Windsor Castle

Windsor Castle is the most
famous castle in England.

It is one of the homes of the Queen.

There has been a castle here since
the time of William the Conqueror.

A German castle
in a forest.

A castle
near Paris.

A Scottish
castle.

A hunting castle
in Italy.

A German castle
on a hill.

A castle
in Holland.

A 13th century castle